FRIGHT NIGHT!

Adapted by Kate Howard

Scholastic Children's Books,
Euston House,
24 Eversholt Street,
London NW1 1DB, UK

A division of Scholastic Ltd
London ~ New York ~ Toronto ~ Sydney ~ Auckland
Mexico City ~ New Delhi ~ Hong Kong

This book was first published in the US in 2016 by Scholastic Inc.
Published in the UK by Scholastic Ltd, 2016

ISBN 978 1407 17205 7

Book design by Rick DeMonico

Printed and bound by CPI Group (UK) Ltd, Croydon, CR0 4YY

2 4 6 8 10 9 7 5 3 1

CONTENTS

From the Files of Merlok 2.0 iv

Chapter 1 1

Chapter 2 17

Chapter 3 27

Chapter 4 42

Chapter 5 51

Chapter 6 64

FROM THE
FILES OF
MERLOK 2.0

Greetings, and welcome to the Files of Merlok 2.0 - that's me! Now where was I . . . ? Ah, yes! For over one hundred years, the kingdom of Knighton knew only peace. In the capital city of Knightonia, humans and Squirebots began to live side-by-side, surrounded by the city's technical marvels - like the awe-inspiring Beam Bridges or the state-of-the-art Joustdome.

I, Merlok the wizard, used my magic to help the kingdom whenever I could. My greatest task was to keep the dangerous Books of Dark Magic locked away in my library. The most wicked of these books was The Book of Monsters. Under my very nose, this clever book plotted to escape from my library.

One day, the book found the perfect puppet for its plans: Jestro, the court jester. Jestro had no friends in the kingdom except for Clay Moorington. Clay tried to be kind to the jester, but everyone else thought Jestro was a joke – and not the funny kind. Jestro was tired of everyone laughing at him instead of with him.

Lonely and eager to prove that he was nothing to be laughed at, Jestro was a perfect target for The Book of Monsters' offer. If Jestro freed it, together they could unleash an evil on Knighton. Soon, the citizens of Knighton would be serving Jestro, not laughing at him.

Jestro and The Book of Monsters launched their attack right away. With a wave of a magic staff over the pages of The Book of Monsters, evil monsters sprang to life.

A team of brave knights banded together to fight them. Clay Moorington and his friends Lance Richmond, Macy Halbert, Aaron Fox, and Axl took up their shields and charged against the monsters. But muscle and iron are no match against magic monsters.

In the end, I was the only one who could stop them. I cast a powerful magic spell to destroy the monsters and . . . *boom!* Jestro and The Book of Monsters were blown far away from the castle. Although the monsters were defeated, my library was also destroyed, and dangerous Books of Evil were scattered across the kingdom.

The explosion also left me trapped as a digital hologram in the castle's computer system. But it isn't all bad. Now, I am able to harness the power of magic and technology together. In this new form I can download magical NEXO Powers to the knights, so they can defeat whatever monsters attack.

Now it's a fair fight. Clay, Lance, Macy, Aaron, and Axl train with their NEXO Weapons and NEXO Shields so they'll always be ready when Jestro and The Book of Monsters attack - and they will! The NEXO KNIGHTS team has only just begun to see what Jestro's monsters can do . . .

CHAPTER 1

The sun was setting when the NEXO KNIGHTS team's rolling castle – the Fortrex – rumbled up to the village of Spittoon. The sky was awash in bright orange and pink streaks, making the village look peaceful and welcoming. But the knights of Avatron knew looks could be deceiving. There were dark powers at work in their usually peaceful land – specifically, Jestro, the court's former jester, and an ancient Book of Monsters. Jestro was using the book to release monsters all over the kingdom. So these five new graduates of the Knights'

Academy were on a quest to try to bring peace and safety back to the Realm of Knighton.

"I sense a great power near the rough-and-tumble town of Spittoon," said Merlok 2.0 from inside his operating system. Once a powerful wizard (with a seriously snazzy wizard's beard, hat, swishy cloak, and the rest of the look), Merlok had recently been sucked into a computer. Now, he existed as a complicated computer program – with some pretty cool digi-magic at his disposal.

Merlok 2.0 was only just getting used to his new powers . . . and his new look. As part of the Fortrex's computer system, Merlok 2.0 was now a bright-orange hologram. With his digi-magic, he was able to help the NEXO KNIGHTS team when they most needed it. He could download NEXO Powers right into their armour. If they needed a specific kind of help during a battle, they could summon Merlok's help and – *ka-pow!* – instant digi-magic fighting powers!

Merlok 2.0 breathed deeply. Though he couldn't actually smell anything from inside his computerized shell, he knew deep breaths and a calm voice always made a person seem wiser. Deep breath in, deep sigh out. The digital wizard's voice rang out over the Fortrex's speaker system as he scanned the village in front of their rolling castle. "I can feel the power surrounding Spittoon in my ancient bones."

Clay Moorington – the most knightly of all the NEXO KNIGHTS heroes – gazed out from the highest tower of the Fortrex. Clay adjusted his blue-and-gold armour and puffed out his chest. "Spittoon is the toughest village in the Realm," he told Merlok 2.0 and Lance Richmond, his fellow knight.

"They spit a lot," Lance noted casually. "It's unsanitary."

Clay ignored the useless information as he squinted out over the village of Spittoon. Lance never took things seriously enough for a true knight, and it frustrated Clay. The Knights' Code told Clay that he must consider their next move carefully. He wished he wasn't the only one in the group who worried about the impression he and the other knights were making on the people of the Realm. Because they had just graduated from the Knights' Academy, the five NEXO KNIGHTS heroes still had a long way to go before they had fully earned the trust and respect of the people of the Realm.

"We're gonna have to make an entrance that impresses them," Clay said. He had a feeling Lance would like this idea – handsome, popular Lance loved nothing more than to make a grand entrance. And because he was the most famous of the knights, Lance absolutely loved being noticed.

Clay turned and spoke to a group of mechanical Squirebots who were anxiously awaiting their orders. "Squires, play the 'Fanfare of Fortitude'." On his command, the band of Squirebots – who called themselves The Boogie Knights – played a regal song. As the music washed over the valley, Clay turned to address the people of Spittoon. "Greetings, citizens of Spittoon! We are the Knights of Knighton, sworn protectors of the Realm."

The people who were gathered below looked up. For a moment, it almost seemed like they were cowering in fear. Then it was clear that they *were* cowering in fear. At the sound of Clay's voice, many of Spittoon's villagers scattered and ran for cover. Inside their homes, the citizens shuttered their windows and doors.

"They seem a bit, um . . . skittish," Merlok 2.0 said.

Lance yawned, then shot Clay an amused smile. "See? You scared them with your boringness, Clay."

"This is supposed to be the toughest village in the Realm?" Clay scoffed.

"Times change," Lance told him. He shrugged arrogantly and added, "You gotta change with them." He nodded at the musical Squirebots. Wiggling his eyebrows, he ordered, "Put a little funk in that fanfare, will ya?"

The Boogie Knights cranked up the funk factor. The band of robots danced and swayed as they blasted their trumpets and lutes.

"Lance," Clay growled. This was not a time for nonsense! "What are you doing?"

Lance shrugged. He knew it would all work out – eventually. When you were Lance, things always did. "I'm working on our entrance, Clay-man. You only get one chance to make a first impression, you know."

"Yes, I do." Clay held out his hand to silence The Boogie Knights' trumpet section. "Which is why I hoped – as per our Knights' Code – we would present ourselves with power, respect and solemn dignity."

Aaron Fox burst out onto the balcony just in time to add, "And no fear!" The most daring of the knights zoomed past the others. Aaron often used his shield as a hoverboard, which really ruffled Clay's armour (Clay wished his fellow knight would realize his shield was *not* a toy!).

With a twist and a backflip, Aaron leapt onto his hover shield and dropped off the side of the balcony tower. Whooping, Aaron blasted away from the Fortrex and soared towards the houses that lined the quiet streets of Spittoon. His snazzy green-and-grey armour was a streak of colour in the darkening sky.

As Aaron raced towards the village, the town roared to life. Many of the villagers who hadn't already hidden away inside their homes screamed and ducked for cover. Aaron zoomed over the tops of houses, his hover shield skimming across rooftops before it delivered him into the centre of the village.

Clay watched the mayhem from above. Suddenly, he realized Aaron wasn't the only one of the knights who had ventured out into Spittoon. Axl, the largest – and hungriest – of the knights had also made his way into the village centre. The enormous knight lumbered through the town like a gentle giant, but the villagers ran from him like he was an ogre! Clay watched him from above, then called out, "Axl!"

But Axl was too distracted by a food cart. As Clay watched from the Fortrex, Axl grabbed a chunk of meat from the vendor's stand. "Boring?" Axl grunted, drooling over the meat. "BOAR-ing!" He gobbled up the chunk of boar in one bite, hardly noticing that the shopkeeper had jumped up and fled when he saw Axl coming. "Yum!" Axl said happily, munching loudly.

"Why are they all so afraid of everything?" Clay wondered aloud as the people of Spittoon scattered. "They should be spitting and grunting and scratching themselves, if memory serves. What do you think, Merlok? Lance?" He turned. Neither the wizard nor Lance was on the balcony with him any more. "Merlok?

Lance?" Clay peered over the tower wall again.

In the village, Lance had managed to find a pack of Squirazzi and a few adoring fans. Lance posed and preened, waiting for the usual happy screams. He *loved* being such a popular guy. Lance blew air kisses at the crowd, waving majestically. But instead of cheering and clapping, the crowds around him fled. They screamed with terror.

"Wow," Lance said, brushing his hair away from his face. "Something really is weird here."

Clay looked around, realizing he was alone – with only The Boogie Knights for backup – at the top of the tower. He shrugged at the band and said, "You might as well go down there, too. Just as long as you take—" But before he could finish his orders, the Squirebots leaped over the edge of the wall and slid into Spittoon. Clay sighed. "...As long as you take the stairs."

The Boogie Knights crashed at the bottom, landing in a tumbled heap of instruments. Clay was furious. Why was he the only one who took this job seriously? "Does anybody remember our plan to make a 'respectful, dignified' entrance?"

"I do, Clay," said Macy Halbert. She strutted out onto the balcony and gazed out over Spittoon. As the king's daughter, Macy understood the words respectful and dignified better than anyone...she just didn't *enjoy* being respectful and dignified when it meant she couldn't also be rough and tumble. Macy wanted nothing more than to have some fierce fun once in a while! "Watch this – and this!" Macy swung her mace around her head, pretending she was deep in battle. Her red ponytail swung through the air as she whipped her powerful weapon around and around. "And some of this!" Macy grunted and swung, eager to impress her fellow knight with her toughness.

"All I can say is ..." Clay broke off suddenly. "Oh no!" Below them, a small child was standing on the edge of a well. She had her arms outstretched, trying to grab a balloon that had escaped from her chubby fingers. The hairs on the back of Clay's neck stood up. It looked like a citizen was in danger – and that meant it was time for a real hero to take action! With a powerful jump, Clay leapt over the edge of the castle wall and slid into the village. He whisked the child out of harm's way just before she toppled into the well.

"Now *that* was awesome!" Aaron cheered. He leaned against his hover shield and cheered. "What's Lance talkin' about? You *totally* know how to make an entrance, Clay!"

"I wasn't 'making an entrance'," Clay huffed. "I was saving this young damsel in distress." He smiled down at the little girl, patting her head gently. "Now run along, little girl. Oh . . . and don't forget your balloon!" He held out the girl's balloon, expecting her to thank him with a grateful smile.

But instead, the girl's mother rushed forward and grabbed her daughter away from the pack of gathered knights. "My baby!" she screeched. "My baby! My baby!"

As the mother and child raced away from the knights, Aaron shrugged one shoulder. Then he reached forward and popped the balloon with a cheeky grin. The few remaining villagers who hadn't yet gone into hiding screamed when they heard the sound of the popping balloon. Then they fled, too. Within seconds, the entire village centre was deserted. The knights were alone.

Clay was totally stumped. He couldn't understand why everyone in the village was running from them in fear. Turning to his fellow knights, Clay asked, "*What* is going on here?"

The five knights returned to the Fortrex Command Centre to discuss the situation with Merlok 2.0. The team's two knights-in-training, Ava and Robin, joined them. Ava and Robin were on a break from their first year at the Knights' Academy. The two junior knights helped the team with tech and computer support when they were out on their missions, hoping someday they would get to join the NEXO KNIGHTS team, too.

The hologram of Merlok 2.0 spoke to all of them all in a serious voice. "Sorcery is going on here."

The knights gazed into their view-screen image of the village. The streets were all still empty, except for one lone villager who was peeking out of his front door. When Axl burped – loudly, so it echoed through the valley – the villager jumped and slammed his door closed again.

"So much for a tough village," Lance said, rolling his eyes.

Ava punched a few buttons on the computer, pulling up a screen with a bunch of graphs. "Whoa," she murmured, her eyes flickering across the screen. "Some of these readings are off the chart. What's going on?"

"It's just as I suspected," Merlok 2.0 said ominously. "There is a Book of Magic. Somewhere in the Dark Woods. It is very powerful. And *very* scary. We need to get this evil book away from the village . . . or Spittoon will be lost to fear for ever."

CHAPTER 2

Deep in the Dark Woods, Jestro – the King's seriously unfunny court jester – was plotting with his newfound evil mentor: The Book of Monsters. Now, The Book of Monsters was no ordinary book. It could talk (too much, Jestro thought), scheme (very well, Jestro admitted), and was filled with dark, magical power. With the right spell, the caster could make evil creatures from the book's pages come to life.

But the knights had defeated Jestro and the book's monsters before. The villains needed to make their monsters stronger, and there was only one way to do that. They had to find the eleven powerful Books of Dark Magic scattered across the Realm and feed them to The Book of Monsters. By eating the magical books, The Book of Monsters would become even more powerful and release some extra-special creeps.

Now, in the Dark Woods, Jestro had stumbled across a new book. And this one looked deliciously sinister.

"Watch it, clown-boy," The Book of Monsters warned as Jestro poked at the mysterious, glowing book with two sticks. "You gotta be very careful. You *don't* want to touch . . . *The Book of Fear!*"

"Yeah, yeah," Jestro muttered. He furrowed his brow as he tried to lift The Book of Fear to get a better look. The jester's painted-on smiley face looked shadowy and cruel in the dark forest. "So it's a spooky book. All I care about is that we beat those goody knights to it." He thrust the creepy book at The Book of Monsters, urging it to gobble it up. "Just open wide and . . . down the hatch."

The Book of Monsters sputtered, "Hey, wait . . . hold – " But Jestro had already shoved The Book of Fear into its mouth. The Book of Monsters chewed it up. Jestro laughed and waved his staff over The Book of Monsters' open pages. "Let's see what kind of monsters this gets us!"

The Book of Monsters burped. Purple smoke filled the air as The Book of Monsters shuddered and glowed. A moment later, three glowing Globlins popped out of The Book of Monsters' pages. All three of the evil flaming-red balls sprouted spider legs, then scurried around the dark forest. They were ready to work their magic fear-power.

The Book of Monsters continued to shake and glow. More purple smoke filled the air. Then a moment later, another ominous creature popped out of the book's pages. She was tall and glowed like hot coals, with a long serpent's tail that slithered across the forest floor. The creature hissed, then flicked a pair of fiery whips into the air. Jestro had never seen anything like her before. She was so terrifying that he took a cautious step backward and hid behind a giant rock.

"Hey, scaredy-pants," The Book of Monsters teased Jestro. "Don't worry about Whiparella here. As long as her whips don't touch you, you'll be fine." Whiparella snapped her shimmering whips all around, narrowly missing Jestro's clownish face. Jestro shrieked in fear, then tried to act cool about it.

"And that hair!" The Book of Monsters

said, gazing at Whiparella. "Love it! Isn't she frightening?"

"Uh, yeah," Jestro agreed. "She's plenty scary. Not to me, obviously, but I can see how she would fill others with fear." He grinned mischievously. He had been looking for just the right creature to torture the NEXO KNIGHTS team. Giggling, Jestro said, "Like those pesky knights! Finally, they will know real fear!"

Nearby, the NEXO KNIGHTS team forged into the Dark Woods on their new quest. They were on the hunt for the powerful book Merlok 2.0 had warned them about. They had no idea Jestro had already found it and summoned some seriously frightful monsters.

"Hey," Macy said, glancing around at the creepy trees surrounding them. Rocks cast shadows over the dark ground, and branches drooped close over their heads. "Do you think we should wait until morning to look for this book?"

"You heard Merlok," Clay said. "We've got to get that thing before Jestro does."

"Why do you wanna wait, Macy?" Aaron teased. "Are you scared?" Aaron and the three other guys chuckled.

Macy scoffed, "No, I'm not *scared*. I just think it would be easier to see in the *Dark* Woods when it's *light* out."

"She sounds scared to me," Lance noted. The other three laughed again.

"Fear not, Macy," Clay said nobly. "There is nothing out here that can frighten us."

In the dark and gloomy forest, none of the knights noticed that Whiparella had slipped out of the shadows. Slowly, quietly, she crept past the knights. Then, with a quick flick of her wrist, she shot one of her whips out and grabbed Clay around the ankle. Tugging with silent stealth, she pulled him into the forest with her.

"Clay!" Macy shouted when she realized their friend was gone. The others skidded to a stop and spun around, searching through the shadows for some sign of Clay. But just like Macy had told them all, it was too dark.

Clay was nowhere to be seen.

"What happened?" Clay moaned when he came to a few minutes later. His eyes were glassy as he gazed into the thick forest. He blinked, unable to clear away all of the magical purple haze that clouded his vision. "Feels like something stung me . . ."

Whiparella smirked from the trees while she watched her magic take hold. Whenever her whips touched someone, that person was overcome with his or her own worst nightmares. Whiparella could figure out her victims' biggest fears and bring them to life! She was cooking up something truly fun for Clay . . .

Clay's eyes focused on the forest around him. He blinked. Then blinked again, finally clearing the purple haze away. He looked into the trees, sure he had seen something strange. Was that—?

"Help!" A woman cried from nearby. As Clay watched, the woman was snatched up and carried away through the forest by a monster! From atop the monster's shoulders, the woman screeched in fear.

Clay leapt to his feet. It was time for him to take action! "Fear not, ma'am! I, Clay Moorington, Knight of Knighton, shall assist you in this dark wood!" He puffed out his chest. He flexed his biceps. He brushed off his armour. He did everything he could to make himself look as knightly as a true knight should.

The damsel rolled her eyes. "Will you just hurry up and save me already? This damsel is in some serious distress!"

Clay charged into the forest – and farther away from the rest of the knights. When there was a damsel to rescue, *nothing* could stand in his way. He raced through the forest, ducking under branches.

"Hurry, brave knight!" The damsel called out. "My captor is getting weary! It shall be with great ease that you do your knight's duty and rescue me now."

"For justice!" Clay bellowed. "For honour! For a damsel!" He raced forward. "There, m'lady! The monster has ... got away?" He scratched his head and looked around. There was no sign of the damsel in distress *or* her captor. How had they escaped him?

A cry came from deeper in the forest. "Help!"

Clay was stumped. He had *never* failed in a rescue mission. And he certainly wasn't about to now. He scratched his chin, perplexed.

Nearby, Jestro and The Book of Monsters watched Clay with great delight. They knew that with Whiparella's magic at work, Clay would *never* save this damsel. And it was going to be great fun to watch his torture. "Oh, yeah!" The Book of Monsters said, laughing. "She found his fear!"

CHAPTER 3

"Is it time to eat yet?" Axl asked, sniffing a stick to see if it smelled like food. The enormous knight poked under a large leaf, looking for any sign of Clay . . . and snacks.

Aaron groaned. "You just had third breakfast."

"Sorry, Axl," Lance told him. "First we find Clay, then we break for, um, first lunch." He headed off into the forest.

Macy called after him, "But I heard something over here." She pointed in the opposite direction.

"Perhaps we should split up," Lance suggested.

"In the Dark Woods?" Macy gasped.

"What . . . are you scared?" Aaron teased.

Macy shook her head. "No, of course not. I'm just saying we should, uh . . . split up and find Clay."

"Great idea," Lance muttered. "Wish I'd thought of that."

The knights all set off in different directions. After walking only a short distance, Axl tipped his head up and sniffed. His nose had caught a whiff of something delicious. But a moment later, Whiparella's whip hit him and Axl was overtaken with The Book of Fear's powers. His eyes glowed purple as the magic set in. "Mmm. Something smells good."

He had no idea Whiparella was lurking in the bushes nearby, and that what he smelled was all just a trick to torture him . . .

Axl followed his nose to a large dinner table that was heaped with food and drinks in the middle of the forest. "So much food!" Axl grunted, his mouth watering. He rushed towards the table, ready to chow down. But just before he got to it, a gang of flaming Globlins shot out of the woods and devoured every last scrap of food on the table. There was nothing left but dirty dishes. It was Axl's worst nightmare – no food! "Nooooooo!" he screamed.

Nearby, Jestro and The Book of Monsters watched the scene with great delight. Jestro giggled. "What a big fraidy cat," he said.

Elsewhere in the woods, Lance strutted proudly. He whistled and kept his shoulders back. He hoped that by trying to look relaxed, he might begin to feel a bit less tense, too. He peeked between two leaves – and got a brief glimpse of Whiparella's glowing whips. He scratched his head, curious about what he had seen . . .

But before he could figure it out, Whiparella snapped her whips at him. She was eager to overpower Lance with her cruel magic. He was hit. Lance swooned.

"Hey, bugs," Lance called out, feeling woozy as Whiparella's magic seeped into him. "Don't bite me . . . I'm a Richmond!" He spun around, but Whiparella had already slipped away. Lance's eyes went fuzzy and glowed purple with the book's magic.

Then a moment later, he brightened. Ahead of him in the forest he spotted Burnzie the monster. The enormous red beast was surrounded by a pack of Squirazzi! The Squirazzi's cameras were flashing like crazy, taking picture after picture of the big, foolish monster. Burnzie grinned and the monster's grotesque teeth glowed white with each flash of the camera.

"Hey!" Lance called out. Cameras always *loved* him. This would be the perfect opportunity for the Squirazzi to catch Lance acting like a true hero. His bravery would be captured on film, and he would be even *more* of a star than he already was! He would certainly be known from now on as the most *famous*, most *brave* knight in all the Realm. "Hey, vile monster! I shall set these noble Squirazzis free." He beamed at the cameras. "Free to take my picture for their celebrity photo spreads, that is!"

Lance lunged forward, striking blow after blow at Burnzie. "Action!" he cried out, naming each pose as he grinned for the cameras. "Glamour! Boy next door!" He raised his lance heroically. "Cover shot!"

After a short fight, Burnzie ran away defeated. Lance spun around, eager to smile and pose for the adoring Squirazzi cameras. But the strangest thing happened: none of them seemed the least bit interested in Lance.

In fact, rather than thanking him, one of the camera guys shouted at Lance. "Hey! You chased off Burnzie, the biggest celebrity in Knighton!"

"*What?*" Lance said, gaping at the Squirazzi. "He's a monster! And I just rescued you! And I'm a *celebrity*!"

"Uh-oh," the camera guy said, rolling his eyes at the other Squirazzi. "Poser alert. Maybe we can still catch Burnzie!" He and the others began to run after the monster.

Lance chased after them. "Hold on! Perhaps you missed this look – I call it . . . *Superstar!*" The forest around him seemed to glow as Lance gave them his most spectacular pose. But no one paid him any attention. Lance was growing desperate and terrified. What if he was – *gulp!* – not popular any more? How could the cameras prefer ugly old Burnzie to *Lance Richmond*? "Hey, come back! I'll give you some shots from my good side!"

On the other side of the forest, Macy trudged through the dense woods. Suddenly, she, too, was hit by Whiparella's whip. Her eyes turned purple as the magic from The Book of Fear seeped into her body. "Hey!" She raised her mace, ready to fight back. Through the trees, the only thing she could see was a huge, glowing red monster. Macy recognized the monster right away. It was Sparkks! The knights had defeated Sparkks many times, and Macy knew she could take the ugly, one-eyed beast down easily. This would be a great chance to show the other knights that she really had what it took to be a hero! "Don't move, monster."

"Or what?" Sparkks hissed. "Gonna hit me with your little flowers? Ooh! Maybe you'll blind me with your shiny dress."

"What?" Macy blurted out. She glanced quickly at her weapon, gasping when she noticed it had turned into a bouquet of flowers! She reached up to touch her helmet, then realized it was no longer on her head. "Hey! Where's my mace? And my NEXO KNIGHTS helmet?"

"A knight?" Sparkks scoffed. "Oh, please. You're no *knight*! You're just some pretty little princess out picking flowers."

Macy lunged for the monster. "Why you – ughh!" She stumbled. Looking down, she could see that her armour had become a *princess dress*! "A sparkly dress? Gah!" Macy swatted at the pale-blue dress covered in flouncy bows and ribbons. What a nightmare! A fussy dress, no helmet, and a bouquet of stinky flowers? What kind of knight carried flowers? Taking another step, Macy stumbled on the hem of her dress and fell to the ground.

"Aw," Sparkks teased. "Did the pretty little princess fall down?"

Very near the place where Macy was trying to battle Sparkks, Clay was still chasing after the damsel in distress. "Gotcha!" he said, lunging towards the woman's captor. But instead of getting a hold on her, he landed empty-handed, flat on his face.

"What is with you?" the damsel shouted at him. "I thought you were a brave and noble knight!" She used a silly voice to copy Clay's earlier words. "*'For justice! For honour!'*" Muttering, she added, "More like . . . for *nothing*!"

Clay grumbled under his breath. He ran towards the woman's captor one more time – but again, he missed both the monster and the damsel in distress completely. "This can't be happening!" he wheezed, falling to the ground.

Just then, Macy stumbled towards him. She tripped on her dress and cried out, "Ahhh!"

"Whoa . . . Macy?" Clay said, gaping at her. "What happened to you?"

Macy looked down at her gown. "Is it that bad?"

"Well, uh, no. I've just never seen you look so . . ." Clay trailed off.

"Pathetic?" Macy prompted.

"Elegant," Clay said.

"Now you're just mocking me." Macy frowned. She grunted and tore at the dress, trying to pry away the annoying costume.

Clay shook his head. "No! I mean, at least you haven't completely failed as a knight. Like me. I can't . . ." He drew in a ragged breath. "I can't even rescue a damsel in distress!"

"Let me help," Macy offered. "I'm as tough and fearless as ever!" She tried to charge forward, but her dress was wrapped too tightly around her legs and she tripped again. Kicking at the fabric, Macy howled, "Stupid dress!"

*

Things were bad for all of the knights. Lost

in the woods, each of them was being tortured by Whiparella's cruel magic. She had poisoned four of them with their own worst nightmares – only Aaron had yet to be hit.

Axl stumbled through the forest, desperate to find food. "Finally!" he said when he came upon another heaped banqueting table in a clearing. "Lunch!"

The enormous knight raced forward, nearly crashing into Lance. Lance was still chasing after the band of Squirazzi, who were obviously eager to get away from him.

"C'mon!" Lance pleaded with the photographers. "Just one picture! I'm Lance Richmond! Everyone loves me!"

"Sorry," one of the camera guys said, spinning around. "Never heard of you."

Lance stomped, throwing a teensy tantrum. "You are so fired when my dad reaches out to your boss!" Lance raced after the cameras again, barely even noticing Axl as he rushed past.

Axl wasn't bothered, though. He only had eyes for one thing: food! Lots of food. He had never been so hungry, and all he wanted was a tiny bite. He charged towards the tables full of treats, howling when Globlins – once again – beat him to it. They dived on top of a pie, munched on a turkey leg, and ate every last scrap of food before Axl could get any! "What? My food!" Unable to stand the torture any longer, Axl began to weep. Big, horrible sobs that rocked the forest around him. He gazed at the table full of munched-on apple cores and empty platters and cried for the food he could still smell.

Suddenly, the Squirazzi rushed into the clearing and snapped pictures of him weeping beside the table.

"Really?" Lance shrieked. "Empty plates rate pictures?"

"Empty plates!" Axl sobbed.

Macy, Clay, Axl and Lance were all utterly miserable. But farther off in the forest, Aaron was still happy and whistling. Little did he know, he was about to come face-to-face with Whiparella!

The glowing monster leaped out of the forest and snapped her whip at Aaron. But he spun around so quickly that he was able to grab her whip in his bare hand. "Hey!" he barked, narrowing his eyes at her. "What gives?"

Whiparella looked at him, shocked. No one had ever caught her before. It was time to come up with a Plan B. "Oh, uh ... *this* is what gives!" Whiparella screamed as she began to grow. While Aaron watched from the forest floor,

Whiparella grew bigger and bigger, until she was towering over him. "And now," she growled. "I will fill you with fear!"

CHAPTER 4

A giant Whiparella loomed over Aaron, cracking her whips. "Does my huge, frightening self scare you, tiny knight?"

Aaron's eyes grew wide as he took in the sight of the enormous glowing beast. "Whoaaaaa," he marveled. "That is *sick*! Do it again. Do it again!"

"What?" Whiparella gasped. "You're not frightened?"

Aaron shook his head. "No way! That looks awesome!"

"Well, then," Whiparella said, considering her next move. "Perhaps you have a fear of heights!" She lashed her whip at the ground and wrapped it around Aaron's body. She lifted him up, up, up – above the treetops, into the clouds.

When he was high in the sky, Aaron hooted and howled. "Woo-hoooooo!" he cheered. Aaron *loved* the thrill of heights. He slipped out of Whiparella's whip-hold and hopped onto his hover shield. Tilting his board, he rode down Whiparella's enormous side, using her glowing body as a giant, monstrous skate park. "Whoa!" Aaron said when he hopped off at the bottom. "Mad props for the ride, Mullet Mary."

Whiparella shrank back down to her usual size and glared at Aaron. "What did you say?" She patted her hair, feeling self-conscious. "This is not a mullet! It's a Dread Lock! And let's see how brave you are now ... around my creepy crawlies!" She waved her hand in the air, and several Globlins rushed towards Aaron. They sprouted spider legs and skittered around his body, hissing at him.

"I am so totally . . ." Aaron said, eyeing the Globlins warily, "buggin' out!" He hopped on his hover shield again, zooming around the spider-Globlins. As he wound through the pack of critters, the Globlins' legs got all tangled up and they fell into a messy heap. The critters whimpered, helpless, while Aaron whooped with joy. "That is so *off da shield*, yo. What else ya got, Chili Pepper Pam?"

"What?" Whiparella yelled. "That is not my name, either!"

Aaron shrugged. "Whatevs, Hot Links Heidi."

Whiparella growled, her anger mounting with each new name Aaron came up with. People did *not* tease Whiparella! "I am

Whiparella!" she howled, flicking her whips in the air. She bared her pointed, fang-like teeth at Aaron, fuming. "With one snap from my whip, I can find your deepest, darkest fear and bring it to life!"

Aaron chuckled. "No way, Whippenstein."

"Yes way!" Whiparella argued. "And it's *Whiparella*! I've crushed all your knight friends. Not with weapons. But with their own worst nightmares." She cackled as she thought about how she'd tortured Axl with delicious food that he couldn't have. "I preyed upon Axl's fear of hunger – the greatest meal, always just out of reach."

Whiparella went on. "Fear of obscurity," she raised her arms in the air, thinking of Lance and how he had pleaded with the Squirazzi to take just one picture of him. "Lance is a spoiled boy in a world that doesn't even care he exists."

She laughed, thinking about how Macy had struggled to move in her fussy, sparkly dress. "I played with Macy's fear of being a princess who shall *never* become a true knight."

And then there was Clay, who was so desperate to prove himself to be a hero. Whiparella cackled. "Clay is overcome by his fear of failing. Not just damsel in distress I created, but he fears failing with your beloved Knights' Code as well."

Aaron nodded, as though he understood. He leaned back against a giant boulder, sucking down a can of fizzy drink. "Good times. Right, *Wimp-arella*?"

"Stop that!" Whiparella screeched. Her yellow eyes glowed with fury. "And tell me why my fear magic has no effect on you? I've got no sense of any fear from you!"

"That's because I've got NO FEAR!"

Aaron roared. He lifted his bow and strummed on it as if it were a guitar, screaming out a rock beat. "None whatsoever. Woo-hoo!" He raised his arms and pumped his fists in the air.

"But that can't be," Whiparella hissed. "Everyone has fears. Some are just less obvious. How about these classics…" She whistled, summoning up more scary things. First, she conjured up a monster standing at a chalkboard. On Whiparella's cue, the creature raked its long, talon-like fingernails across the board. A horrible screeching noise echoed through the forest. Whiparella covered her ears – the sound was horrible!

But Aaron loved it. "Ooh! Lemme play some harmony!" He pulled out his bow-guitar and jammed along with the music of the nails on the chalkboard.

Whiparella frowned. Then she got

another idea. She grinned. "Everyone fears the dentist!" She shoved Aaron into a huge dentist's chair, cackling as the dentist hovered over him with a whizzing dental drill.

"Woo!" Aaron cheered from inside his seat. "Nothin' to fear. I got *no* cavities. I'm a big brusher, yo. 'Cause plaque is whack!" He opened his mouth wide, letting the dentist have at him.

Whiparella was growing more and more frustrated with each failed attempt. "*Hmm. Ha!* The naked truth! That never fails to destroy you!" With a quick flip of her hand, Whiparella zapped the clothes and armour right off Aaron's body.

Holding his shield in front of himself, Aaron glanced around the forest nervously. "Whoa, where did my armour go?"

Whiparella laughed. "You're completely exposed for all the world to see. Nowhere to hide now. Within moments you'll be—"

Aaron strutted proudly through the clearing. He announced, "I'm rockin' the commando look!"

"What?!" Whiparella growled.

"I've never felt so free!" Aaron told her. "Thanks, Whipper-Snapper."

Whiparella howled. She was *furious*! And she was also out of ideas. She stormed off to plot her revenge.

Aaron had stopped Whiparella from capturing him, but he still needed help to save his friends. *If only there was a NEXO Power that could make the other knights, um, unafraid . . .*

As if in answer to Aaron's thoughts, he heard Merlok 2.0's voice through his shield. "Prepare for NEXO Scan!"

This was exactly what Aaron needed! He raised his shield in excitement. "NEXOOOOO Knight!" he called.

"NEXO Power: Lion of Bravery!" Merlok 2.0 announced.

A moment later, Aaron's shield surged with new power as the NEXO Power downloaded. Aaron lifted his shield, sending beams of white, magical light out into the dark forest. Then he raced through the woods. It was time to save his friends from their worst nightmares!

CHAPTER 5

Nearby, Clay had grown weak with the effort of trying to rescue the damsel in distress. He crawled through the forest, trying to catch the woman and her captor. Macy followed close behind.

"Please, monster," he begged, gasping for breath. The monster raced in circles around him, the woman clutching the monsters shoulders so she wouldn't fall off. Clay reached out to them, begging, "Stop ... I must save the damsel. Or else ... my honour, my chivalry ... all that matters." His voice broke. "I have failed."

Aaron burst out of the woods at that moment. Waving his shield proudly, he cried, "You talkin' about *this* damsel?" He shot two arrows – one at the monster, and one at the damsel in distress. The monster dissolved the moment the arrow struck.

While Clay watched, horrified, the woman hissed ... and then she, too, morphed into a monster! She had been a creature disguised by Whiparella's powers all along. Aaron shot another arrow at the creature, then whooped when it dissolved. "Boo-ya!"

"Aaron?" Clay said, looking from the two monsters to his fellow knight. "What are you doing here?" His eyes bulged out of his head, then he looked down, embarrassed. "And where's your armour?"

Aaron glanced down at his still-naked body. With a casual shrug, he explained,

"Ah, some whip lady took 'em. I think she was trying to scare me."

"Well, uh," Clay cringed. "Honestly, your lack of modesty is scaring me a bit."

Aaron grinned. "Oh ... sorry. Be right back." He dashed through the woods, returning a moment later wearing a full set of green-and-grey armour.

"Aaron," Clay asked. "Tell us more about this 'whip lady'?"

"Oh," Aaron said. "Well, she snaps you with her whip and your worst fears come to life."

"What?" Macy asked. Everything that had happened in the woods was suddenly starting to make more sense.

Aaron proudly added, "But I have no fear! Woo-hoo! So it was just kinda fun for me."

"We must find the others," Clay told Aaron and Macy. "But ... the fear."

Aaron shook his head. "Hey, no sweat, bro. You still probably got her scary magic in ya. No worries. I'll take the lead."

Clay nodded gratefully, then he and Macy followed Aaron deeper into the forest. By the time they reached Axl, the huge knight was completely exhausted – and starving.

"So hungry," he moaned. He grabbed for another drumstick on the table. But a Globlin got hold of it at the same time and the creature and Axl played tug-of-war with the chunk of meat. "Please," Axl begged, his body collapsing from hunger. "One bite . . ."

Suddenly, one of Aaron's arrows zipped into the clearing. When it struck the drumstick, the meat dissolved into nothing. Aaron soared into the clearing on his hover shield and batted at the Globlins with his bow. The little monsters scattered. One by one, Aaron hit each of them with arrows and the creatures turned into dust.

Now, the only one left to save was Lance. As Aaron, Axl, Macy and Clay came upon their famous friend in the forest, they could hear him begging. "C'mon," Lance pleaded with the Squirazzi. "Please! I'm Knighton's most celebrated celebutante."

"What'd you say your name was?" one of the photographers asked.

"Lance! Lance Richmond!"

"Oh," the Squirazzi said. "Yeah, never heard of you."

Before Lance could respond, Axl came crashing through the trees. Aaron released one of his arrows, and the first Squirazzi disappeared in a *poof*! One by one, the rest followed. Lance grabbed one of their cameras and took pictures as his fellow knights bashed the magical monsters. The camera flashed just as one of the Globlins was conked over the head. Lance cheered, "Now *that's* what I call a 'cover shot'!"

While the knights celebrated their victory, Whiparella returned to Jestro and The Book of Monsters for further instructions. She told Jestro about her encounter with Aaron, feeling embarrassed that she had failed. She hung her head as she told him how she had failed – all thanks to Aaron.

"What do you mean he had 'no fear'?" Jestro wailed.

"Every one of them crumbled before the terror of their own worst nightmares," Whiparella told him. She lowered her voice to add, "Except the archer. My magic didn't work. He was afraid of *nothing*."

Jestro spun around and screamed at The Book of Monsters. "Are you kidding me? I thought you said she could scare anyone?"

The Book of Monsters asked, "Did you try the creepy crawlers?"

Whiparella nodded.

"What about the dentist?" The Book of Monsters said.

Whiparella nodded again. Sulking, she said, "I even gave him an 'out-of-clothes experience'."

The monsters gathered around in the forest all gasped. Sparkks asked, "Completely naked? In public?"

"Yikes!" Sparkks yowled. "Talk about nightmares!"

The Book of Monsters grumbled, "Wow. I hate the dentist. But that didn't even faze him, huh?"

"No," Whiparella whined. "He called me all kinds of names, like 'Hot Links Heidi' and . . ." She sniffed. "'Wimp-arella.'"

The other monsters all gasped again.

"Aww," Sparkks said sadly, patting her on the shoulder. "That's terrible."

The Scurrier who had spent the whole night torturing Clay chimed in. "It doesn't even make any sense!"

Burnzie shook his head. "You poor thing. Do you need a hug?"

Whiparella nodded gratefully, and all her monster pals squeezed her into a friendly hug.

The Book of Monsters whispered, "'Wimp-arella'? That's pretty good."

Jestro growled at the book and the creatures. "Stop that! All of you, stop that! There will be none of that while I'm here! *No hugging* until we stop those knights! That Aaron must have *something* he's scared of."

"Yeah," came a voice from the woods. It was Aaron! He added, "I'm scared of your terrible comedy routines, Jestro."

Jestro turned just in time to see the knights marching towards him, ready for battle. Jestro shouted, "Now's your chance, Whiparella! Hit him with everything you've got!"

Whiparella looked up from the hug. Her eyes narrowed. She flicked her whips. Then she hissed, "Yes! I don't believe *anyone* fears nothing!" Her whips glowed with magic as she swung both of them at Aaron. She put all her strength into the attack.

But Aaron was ready. He fired back with two arrows. Each one hit one of her whips, sending them backward – straight towards Jestro!

With a *smack*, they hit the evil court jester right in the face. Jestro frowned as the whips' magic sunk in. His eyes glowed. He wobbled and tried to focus on the forest around him. "Uh . . ." he asked, woozy. "Was that supposed to happen?"

"Whoa," The Book of Monsters gasped, cringing. "You were hit with double snaps! Things might get a little scary."

Jestro swayed as the magic took hold. He blinked, and when his droopy eyes opened again, he was back in the Joustdome at the castle. He was on stage, performing for everyone. "Wait," he mumbled aloud. He wasn't sure if he was in the forest or the castle. It was the most real dream he'd ever had! "Where am I?"

The Book of Monsters told him, "Don't worry: you're just in the middle of a very severe fear-dream."

Jestro could hear The Book of Monsters speaking to him, but the voice sounded far away. He looked around the Joustdome, staring nervously up into the stands filled with jeering crowds. He muttered,

"But ... but, I'm in the Joustdome. The last time I looked like a fool. And there are knights here, too. Aaron ..." He blinked and swayed. "Oh, I get it! Aaron said the only thing he feared was my terrible comedy routine. So now ... I shall destroy him!" He stood up and lunged for Aaron. But suddenly, the only thing he could see was people – laughing at him. Everyone was making fun of him!

"Uh," The Book of Monsters told him, "Aaron was only joking about that before. This is actually *your* worst nightmare."

"It is?" Jestro whispered. He glanced around again. All he could see was a sea of faces, and they were all laughing at him.

In the dream, people were screaming, "This guy's awful!" and "He's the worst jester ever!"

Jestro covered his head. "No! This can't be happening. Not again ... keep it together!" Suddenly, he was holding a sword, a mace, a halberd and some arrows. While everyone watched, Jestro tried to juggle them – but they all just rained down around him. He spun plates on sticks, but they all crashed and broke on the Joustdome floor. "Nooooo!" Jestro moaned, then dropped to the ground. He closed his eyes, hoping to hide from the scene inside the nightmare.

The evil jester curled into a ball on the forest floor, his body twitching with fear. All of his monsters leaned over him, waiting for him to wake up from his nightmare.

"Uh ..." Macy said, staring at Jestro wide-eyed. "Is he okay?"

The Book of Monsters gazed down at its master – then looked at the knights. "Yeah," the book said. "But now it's *my* worst fear. We've lost again." The Book of Monsters screamed at the other creatures.

"Grab him! And let's scram!" Sparkks and Burnzie snatched Jestro off the forest floor. Then the book, all the monsters, and Jestro fled in fear.

CHAPTER 6

y the next morning, everything had gone back to normal in the village of Spittoon. Now that The Book of Fear was gone, the knights were quickly able to restore order to the tough town. People were spitting and snarling at each other, just like the good old days.

"Watch your step!" one guy screamed.

"Have a terrible day," yelled another.

When the Fortrex rolled out of town, the villagers waved their fists and spat and pushed one another around some more. It was life as usual in Spittoon – and the knights were off on their next adventure.

"I still think we should have chased after them and . . . *wham*!" Aaron said, slamming his fist into the palm of his hand. He couldn't believe they had let Jestro and The Book of Monsters get away without a fight!

Clay shook his head. "The Knights' Code says we're supposed to defend the downtrodden. Jestro seemed pretty down." He thought back to the previous night, cringing at the memory of his failed rescue. Even though it had all been a dream, it had been a *terrible* dream, and Clay couldn't stop thinking about how he had failed to save the damsel in distress. "But then, I utterly failed the whole 'Knights' Code' thing, didn't I?"

Macy patted him on the shoulder. "Aw, c'mon. Don't be so hard on yourself, Clay. We all fell for that slithery monster's tricks."

"Not Aaron," Clay said. "The Fear Monster looked for his deepest fear and all she found was *nothing*."

Merlok 2.0 cut in, "Ah, but sometimes 'nothing' is the greatest fear of all."

Clay looked stumped. "Sorry, Merlok 2.0, but that makes no sense. Aaron is the truest of knights."

"I suggest you read your Knights' Code again, Clay," said Merlok 2.0. "It says: 'We are many, we are one.'"

Macy nodded. "Yeah, and that means we're a team. We've each got our own strengths that make the team stronger. And it makes each of us stronger, too."

Clay considered this for a moment. He wasn't so sure he agreed.

But Macy went on, "The truest of knights – like *you*, Clay – should understand that."

Clay sighed. Sure, working as a team

was important. But he also worried that he wasn't as tough as he ought to be. He was on a quest to be the best. "Yes, Macy," he said. "But I don't know. I still wish I was like Aaron – afraid of nothing!"

Merlok 2.0 raised his eyebrow. He stroked his beard. Suddenly, he had an idea. It was time to show the knights that *everyone* had a fear – you just had to find it. A moment later, the computerized hologram faded away. Then the castle slammed to a stop and all the power went out. Aaron crashed to the ground when even his hover shield powered down.

"Hey," Aaron said from the floor. "What gives?"

Ava punched at buttons on the computer, trying to power everything back up. "Sorry," Ava said, shrugging. "Some kind of power surge. Merlok 2.0 is offline."

"Is he okay?" Clay asked, concerned.

"He's fine," Robin told the more experienced knights. "But we'll have to shut down everything in the castle to get him back up and running again."

"Even my shield?" Aaron said, a note of panic creeping into his voice.

"No choice," Robin shrugged. "We've gotta make sure there's no electrical interference while we reboot."

"Yeah," Ava agreed. "The system is very fragile. So stay completely silent and still during the reboot. Do *nothing*!"

"What?" Aaron shrieked. He began to tremble. In a whisper, he asked, "But, but . . . how am I supposed to stay still? How long will this take?"

Quietly, Robin told him, "According to this message from Merlok, it will take about ten minutes."

"I have to do *nothing*?" Aaron screamed. "For a whole *ten minutes*?" His eyes went wide, and he began to sweat. He was shaking and trembling.

Lance cocked an eyebrow. "Everything okay, Aaron?"

Aaron shuddered. He was so overcome by the idea of doing nothing that he wasn't even able to speak. "Uhh," he moaned. His body began to twitch and his face was filled with terror. "Ugh . . . not moving. I can't take *nothing*! Ahhhhh!" He threw his arms up in the air and screamed. He ran from the room and the other knights were left to stare after him.

A moment later, the system roared to life again. The hologram of Merlok reappeared – and the wizard was smirking.

"What was *that* all about?" Clay asked.

"Oh," Merlok said, chuckling. "You just saw Aaron's greatest fear: when there is nothing to do. As The Fear Monster said, he is literally afraid of . . . *nothing*!"

"Really?" Macy said. It seemed so silly – and impossible.

"No one is completely fearless, Clay," Merlok said. "Not even the truest of knights."

Clay nodded, finally understanding. He grinned at their trusty wizard adviser. "Merlok . . . you didn't have anything to do with that system reboot, did you?"

The orange hologram of a wizard shrugged. "What? Me?" The corners of his moustache lifted in a smile. "Uh, no . . . I'm a wizard. Not a rebooting, techno-mathingy guy who just happened to bump into a few switches here and there that go beep beep boop."

Macy's mouth hung open. She lifted one eyebrow and whispered to Clay, "What is he talking about?"

Merlok 2.0 continued to make beeping sounds while the rest of the knights shook their heads, confused.

"I don't know," Clay said. "I'm afraid to ask. Very afraid."

Macy nodded and laughed. "We all are sometimes, aren't we?"

Macy and Clay exchanged a smile. Merlok 2.0 continued to *beep* and *boop*, while Axl settled in at a table to eat until he was stuffed. Lance brushed his hair and smiled at himself in the mirror. And Aaron hopped onto his hover shield and raced around the castle, relieved that he hadn't been forced to spend ten minutes doing nothing. The thought was far too terrifying!

As the Fortrex rolled on towards the knights' next adventure, it seemed that things were back to normal – for now. But even as they all relaxed into their favourite activities, the NEXO KNIGHTS team had no doubt their next quest would find them soon. And they would be ready. Separated and alone, the knights had given in to their fears. But as a team they were strong enough to overcome any scary challenge. Together, they would restore harmony to the Realm and defeat Jestro and his monsters once and for all!